Amalgamated

BECCA SEYMOUR

AMALGAMATED

BECCA SEYMOUR

RAINBOW TREE PUBLISHING

For information, contact the author:
authorbeccaseymour@gmail.com

Editing: Hot Tree Editing

Publisher: Rainbow Tree Publishing

Ebook ISBN: 978-1-925853-50-6

Paperback: 978-1-922679-12-3

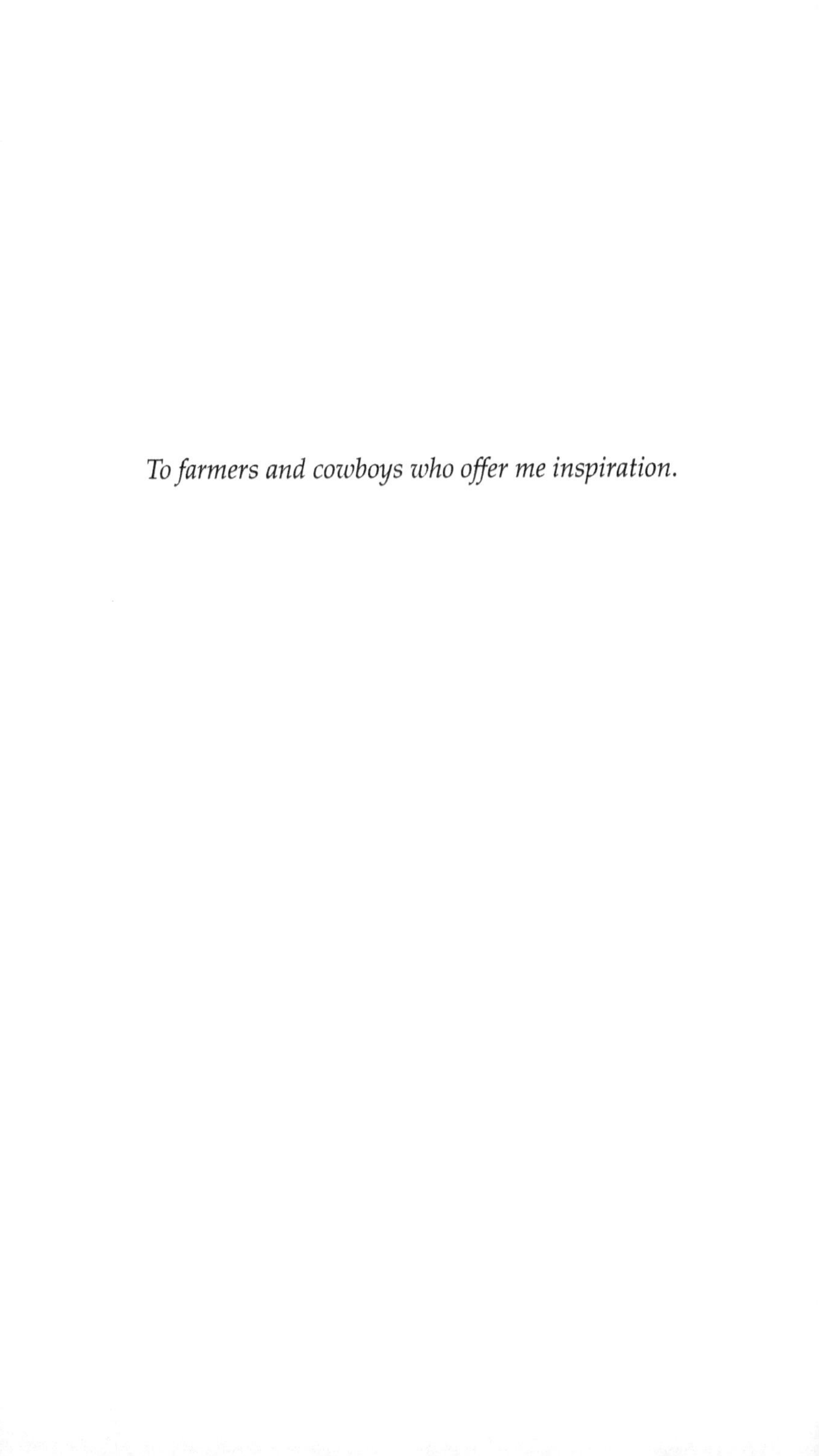

To farmers and cowboys who offer me inspiration.

CHAPTER 1

I flipped off the tap and grabbed a couple of paper towels, relieved they were available rather than a hand dryer. I had an aversion to the damn things. After patting myself dry, I stood up straight. Pleased I'd decided to spend a night in the airport hotel after my international flight before this shorter domestic one, I nodded at my reflection.

It had been a long-arse time since I'd been home—five years pretty much to the day. I shouldn't care what anyone might think of me. I frowned at myself, calling bullshit. There was no "anyone." There was a "he."

Wasn't there always?

I shook my head derisively, unable to lie to myself. And wasn't that a kicker? If I couldn't even do that—pretend that I wasn't so damn eager and equally terrified about seeing Zak again—how in the hell would I behave when I actually came face-to-face with him after all this time? It was inevitable we'd be thrown together at some point.

With a calming exhale, I let my mind continue on the dangerous path of Zak, wondering whether he'd appreciate the good shape I was in, the care I took in my appearance. It shouldn't matter, but it did. And I really wished it didn't. But still, after this shorter internal flight, I felt fresh and ready to get this visit over with.

Armed with my small case, I extended the handle and moved out of the restroom. Jenny was waiting for me, so preparing myself any better was a luxury I didn't have.

The dry heat hit me first; next was a shorter figure complete with strong arms that wrapped me up. My big sister always gave the best of hugs, and after three years since last seeing her—the last time she'd visited me in the UK—her arms felt so damn comforting.

"Hey, you big oaf." Jenny gave one tighter embrace before releasing me and stepping back. "You're a sight for sore eyes, kiddo. Damn, I've missed you, Leo."

I grinned down at her like a loon before tugging her back to me and giving her another fierce hug and planting a kiss on top of her head. "Missed you too, Jen."

She sighed; I assumed feeling the same relief as I was from being close to her again. The moment of quiet contentment lasted approximately another five seconds before she dug her annoying fingers deep into my sides and flexed.

I grunted and fought my squirm and laughter. "Hell, Jen, stop already." I jolted out of her arms. "I'm gonna kick your arse, you know that, right?"

She cocked her hip at me, her palm pressed against it and her brow raised. "You think you can take me?"

I snorted. "I know I can."

"Ha!" She looked me up and down and wrinkled her nose. "I know you look fit enough, but I can bet whatever the hell you damn want, all those measly muscles are gym created rather than hard-labour earned."

I rolled my eyes at her. It was hardly like in my position I was doing hard labour. I was stuck studying samples and attached to my computer most of the day. "Your point?"

Her smart mouth lifted into a smug smile. There'd been so many times as a kid I'd wished for a brother instead of Jenny. But still, I didn't expect a brother would have fought any more fiercely than she had the times she'd stopped bullies; nor did I expect a brother would have given me humiliating, albeit sage, advice on how to give good head when I'd turned sixteen. With that in mind, I figured it was a good job I'd kept her as a sister. I had considered selling her on eBay a time or two. Who was I kidding? I actually did it once, and sported a black eye for a week when she'd found out.

But still, annoying or not, a terrifyingly strong left hook or not, she was Jen, and I couldn't imagine being in a world without her.

"It means you'll be on your back gasping for air after two minutes."

I quirked my brow at her.

"Piss off." She rolled her eyes. "Stop being a weirdo perv."

I laughed. "I didn't say a word."

She huffed. "You didn't have to, tadpole."

My fingers found her sides quickly. I struck hard and fast as I dug my fingers in and made her squeal like a girl, which I promptly told her.

"Get off. And girls are kick-arse, so I can squeal all I damn well want." She eyed my small case, but seemed to think better than to make a comment. Instead, she said, "Do you need help with that? Wouldn't want you to break a nail."

I flipped her the middle finger, then tucked my

hand quickly away, not wanting her to study it and figure out that every few weeks, I actually did have a manicure. In my defence, hand massages were the bomb. No lie. They managed to whip away a stressful day within minutes; plus, even nails looked good. "Where have you parked?"

"Just out the front. Best get a move on before Jed gives me a ticket."

I snorted. If Jed was on patrol, there was no way in hell he'd risk giving Jenny a ticket. As many in our small town knew, messing with the mayor's wife was a no-no.

Once safely seated and buckled in, we headed out of the small airport and made our way towards the outskirts of town where she lived with her husband, Frank. Our mum had long since abandoned the place. When I'd been seven, I'd watched from the veranda as she'd thrown me one last glance before driving off in a plume of dust. It had taken a while for the emptiness to make sense, and even longer for Dad to convince me that Mum loved both Jen and me but she hadn't been well enough to care for us.

Watching the streets go by, a smile lifted my lips. So much was the same, despite the few new stores that had shot up in our small hometown, but Old Jack's, one of the cafes, was still up and running, and the five pubs seemed to still be open to the small community. I shook my head, amused. Five pubs in a town as tiny as ours. It just went to show there was pretty much jack shit to do in the area.

"What?"

A quick glance at my sister, and I smiled. "It's just good to be back, you know?"

She bobbed her head, her eyes flashing to mine a moment before returning to the road. I quirked my brow in response. A quiet Jen was a weird Jen. With no jibes, no sarcasm, hell, even the lack of a quick jab to my side filled me with suspicion that was laced with unease.

"What?"

With her gaze straight ahead, her shoulders dropped just a little, but I knew her better than that. Her attempt to relax was forced. "What do you mean *what*?" Jen's voice was worryingly casual.

I turned a little, staring hard at her head. Silent, I remained still, aiming my gaze at her. I knew all the tricks to get her to spill. Not *that* much had changed over the years.

"Stop it." She flicked a glance my way. "I mean it."

The stare intensified, and I squinted a little.

"For real?"

Jen was close to breaking. I bit the inside of my

cheek, determined not to laugh. She professed to be such a hardarse, yet she was so easy to break.

"Okay." She sighed dramatically. "Promise you won't be mad."

Groaning, I shook my head. Any request starting that way was going to result in me being pissed off. "What did you do?"

This time her glance my way had me tensing. Concern flickered in her eyes. When she focused on the road ahead, she blew out her cheeks, her lips pursed. "We're heading to mine."

"Okay?" I dragged out the word. I'd figured that out since we weren't heading towards Dad and Michelle's.

"Dad kinda got excited about you coming home."

My stomach dipped. I just knew where she was heading with this. Slamming my eyes shut, I waited for her next words.

They came out in a rush. "Sohekindainviteda-heapofpeopleover. But…" She gasped for breath. "… it's not technically a party, as there aren't banners or balloons."

My eyes sprang open, and I stared at her wide-eyed.

She glanced at me, a mix of horror and amusement on her face. "You owe me big for talking him out of *that*."

"Yet you couldn't have talked him into a small family meal?"

She shrugged. "I did try, but, Leo." She paused, emotion swirling in her eyes, and I swallowed. This was just one of the reasons I'd stayed away. Guilt still clawed at me whenever I gave it life. "Dad was so excited you were coming home. You know he still doesn't understand why you left. If it had just been heading to the city, that would have been a struggle, but you travelled to the other side of the world."

My gut clenched. I still felt shit for leaving my dad, but I had my own life to live, and taking over my dad's stud farm wasn't what I wanted. Plus there was the major screw-up with how I destroyed any semblance of a friendship with Zak.

"There's more."

I flashed Jen a resigned look.

"Dad obviously invited Zak."

My heart seized, and my gut churned. This could not be happening. While I'd anticipated seeing him, I wasn't prepared for it to be the first night I got home. In hindsight, this was ridiculously naïve of me, considering his place was only a hundred metres or so away from the main house on the property.

"I know, I know, but best to get the whole awkwardness out of the way, right?" She reached out and gave my hand a small squeeze. After I'd run out on Zak the night I'd left, it had taken just a handful of calls from Jen for her to recognize something was wrong and for me to spill my guts. We remained close, even with the distance of the past five years, and without her in my corner, life certainly would have been trickier.

"Yeah, I suppose." There was something to be said for ripping the Band-Aid off, but my heart picked up speed in anticipation.

The history between Zak and me was complicated. He was eight years older than me, which was no big deal now at twenty-seven, but when I was growing up spending too many nights to count jacking off to the image of him swimming in the creek, I'd known all too well that nothing could ever happen between the two of us. I'd been fifteen when I'd first admitted my feelings to myself, my attraction to him, and was even younger when I first started following him around like a lost lamb.

He was the farm manager and had worked for Dad for years. My dad had trained him up himself and helped him through his studies at uni. It meant that Zak had always been present in my teenage years, was there for breakfast, for dinner, and would regularly be on our veranda after a long day before heading to the workers' cottage.

Looking out at the road ahead, I saw our turnoff

in the distance. I needed to get my head on straight and focus on seeing Dad and enjoying spending time with him. That's what was important.

I chanted that mantra while visualising beer teamed with a couple of shots to get me through this impromptu party with the family I loved, a town I begrudgingly missed, and the man I'd declared my love to before I'd destroyed his prized possession, before I ran off like a fair dinkum coward.

Shit, I'd been a wank stain. It was time to face the music.

CHAPTER 2

.

With a firm handshake, I said my thanks to the Mattersons. I'd lost count of how many familiar faces I'd seen. I was exhausted, but despite my desire for a quiet family dinner when I'd been chauffeured to my sister's, I'd had a good night and had fun catching up with so many old friends and neighbours. There were only a handful of people left. A few of my old high school buddies, my sister and Frank, and my dad and stepmum, Michelle.

Beer had relaxed me enough to kick back on my sister's veranda, but not enough that I could ignore the swirl of unease in my gut.

He hadn't shown.

While I should have been relieved, that was the furthest thing from what I felt. He'd turned down Dad's invite. Yeah, it had been five years, but Zak was always included in everything and pretty much worshipped the ground Dad walked on, so for him to be a no-show said more than his words ever could. Not only that, Dad was confused. While he knew the destruction I'd left in my wake when I'd bailed, I'd never told him the reasons why. And I'd assumed nobody else had, but what did I know? At the end of the day, Zak was entitled to still be pissed off with me. He had every right to stay far away and not have to put on a bullshit front that he was happy to see me.

It was what I deserved.

And while the unease swirled and grew as I wondered what would happen when we did see one another, the pissant in me couldn't be happier that Dad was none the wiser. It didn't matter how old I was, being in Dad's bad books was no joke.

"You okay?"

I glanced over at my sister. A slight frown dipped her brow, and her head tilted in obvious concern.

I nodded and swigged the last drops of my beer. "A bit bolloxed but good. You?"

The frown marring her otherwise smooth forehead eased, and she smiled. "I am. I'm so glad you're here." She reached out her hand, and I took it, giving her a squeeze. I didn't care how much of a hardarse she pretended to be, she was a legit softie.

I leaned back and placed my empty bottle down. "Me too." There were no firm plans for my visit home other than it had been a damn long time since I'd visited and my dad had thrown a stink, complaining I was losing my accent so I'd better get my arse on home soil before I sounded like a Brit. I smirked at the thought. Nobody back in the UK thought I sounded anything Brit-like. I was still Aussie all the way.

"Dad said that he received a call from Zak."

My heart thundered at the mention of his name. "Yeah?"

Jen bobbed her head; her concerned frown was back. "Said one of the mares was fretting."

I bit the inside of my cheek, willing myself to not react. "Problem?" The word came out surprisingly even.

She shrugged, her gaze firmly on me. "There's a few more weeks till she should be foaling."

Perhaps it was a legitimate reason to stay away. Perhaps not. Either way, I had to face him at some point and get through the awkwardness. It was up to me to sort this out. Not make it right, as I didn't think that was possible. But I could start by making the move and apologising.

Exhaling a heavy breath, I looked over to Dad and saw him gathering his things. Jen had already said she'd made a room up for me, but with Dad heading back and with liquid courage thrumming through my system, it seemed like tonight was as good a night as any to get this handled.

"You not staying?" Jen's voice startled me, and I flashed my eyes at her. Her smirk greeted me.

With a shake of my head, I snorted. "No damn idea how you do that, but yeah." I stood and tugged Jen up to give her a hug goodbye. "Thanks for tonight." I placed a kiss on her temple.

"You didn't hate it?"

I shook my head and pulled away, the smile on my face genuine. "I had a good time. It was great catching up."

"But a quiet family dinner tomorrow, right?"

"That'd be great." I glanced at my dad and saw him heading my way. When he stepped to Jen's side, I said, "I'll head back with you tonight."

A large smile appeared on his face, and he nodded. "Sounds good. Michelle will be happy." He draped an arm around my sister's shoulders and placed a kiss on her head. "See you tomorrow at six, kiddo." She nodded. "Love you."

"Love you too." She grinned up at him and then turned to say goodbye to Michelle. I took the time to say goodbye to my brother-in-law and the few stragglers, then made my way out to my dad's ute.

It didn't take long to travel the few kilometres to Dad and Michelle's place. While it was dark, so I couldn't see the familiar sight of home, warmth settled in my chest as we bounced down the long driveway to the main house. There were a few more potholes, but it still felt the same. I released a happy sigh, not quite surprised that it felt good to be home after such a long time, more like content.

I'd loved spending time in the UK. It was pretty ideal; not only hopping over to so many amazing countries in Europe, but for such a small island, there seemed something different to see every time I stepped away from the office. I'd made it my mission to explore and see as much of Europe as I could, knowing it was an opportunity I'd be a fool to pass up on. The reality was that I couldn't imagine being away from home forever, and seeing my family, my friends, and the town I loved sparked a longing in my gut that took me unawares.

I pushed the feeling aside as I stepped outside. Lights filtered from the large stables in the distance. Maybe Zak hadn't come up with a bullshit excuse after all.

"I best head over and check everything is all right." Dad's deep voice tore my gaze away. "Will you help Michelle with the leftovers?"

I bobbed my head. "Of course."

Dad gave me a wink and pressed a quick kiss on Michelle's cheek. "I'll be quick."

The sound of his footsteps on gravel accompanied him. My gaze followed for a few seconds before I turned to Michelle and smiled. "Best get these inside." I tilted my head towards the boot load of food.

She wedged the flyscreen door open as I passed her by with an armful of food. "Just pop them on the kitchen counter, and I'll get everything sorted."

"No worries." I switched the light on with my elbow and was greeted by the familiar kitchen. The large oak table still filled the eating area just off the side of the huge kitchen. A pile of fruit sat in the bowl, and one section of the table was covered in paperwork. It was pretty much the exact image I'd left with.

"I'll throw a plate together for Zak. He must be hungry and exhausted."

I glanced over at Michelle. She was already organising everything, which she did amazingly well. From the moment I'd first met her when I'd been barely a teen, she'd won us all pretty much over with her ability to take charge and sort us all out. It helped that she cooked well and gave the best of hugs. Lord knew I'd made up for years of being motherless by taking advantage of every single one.

My dad had won the damn lotto when she'd agreed to marry him and take us on. I had zero idea how he'd managed it, but I was grateful he had.

"I just need to grab my bag out of the car, then I'll give you a hand."

"Perfect," she answered. "Take it right up to your room. Your dad will only trip over it else. I swear that man doesn't look where he's going half of the time."

A snort left my mouth, and I grinned. "Some things never change, right?"

Michelle paused what she was doing and turned her focus solely on me. With a tilt of her head, she appeared to take me in a moment before speaking. "Right." She nodded. "And sometimes they change for the better, even the people right in front of us, filling up our lives."

I quirked a brow. Was she saying I'd changed? Well, if so, at least it seemed for the good, but to be honest, I was sure I was the same kid who'd left five years ago. Yeah, older, and I hoped a little wiser, but still….

"When you've finished, you can take this out to Zak for me. Maybe seeing you will make him stop for half an hour and actually take a break and eat."

I worked hard to swallow softly, not only at the mention of his name but at the pointed look my stepmum gave me. With a small smile and a forced laugh, I replied, "Well, there's one guy who I'm sure will never change." From the years of knowing him, from growing up and becoming a man around him, the only changes I'd seen in the guy were a result of my infatuation.

Michelle pursed her lips and gave a short nod. "A lot can happen in five years, Leo. Even grown men can make mistakes. Hell, some can even do so and admit they were wrong." She gave a chin lift towards the door. "Go on, get to it. This'll be ready in ten minutes."

I backed out of the room, my mind struggling to catch up. It was not like Michelle to talk in riddles, so her weird comments threatened to addle my jet-lagged brain. Admittedly, it had been a while since I'd seen her and Dad, but we did FaceTime regularly. I could only assume I was reading into something that wasn't there, no doubt hypersensitive about Zak being just a short distance away and knowing in ten minutes I'd be seeing him again.

With that thought driving me forward, I dragged my feet to get my bag inside. No one said excitement couldn't be trumped by fear. And between the two emotions, I was still struggling to figure out exactly how to approach the man who'd stolen my heart so many years ago.

CHAPTER 3

Armed with a plate of chicken, potato salad, and a hunk of bread, I met Dad at the door of the stables just as he was heading out. "Hey, all okay?"

He greeted me with a pat on the shoulder and a wide smile. "She seems to have settled. Zak's just getting ready to leave too." He glanced down at the covered plate. Shaking his head, he chuckled. "You know, I lost count how many times you both would eat out here rather than at the table."

A smile curled my lips. It was the truth. When Zak was knee-deep in training or dealing with something that needed his attention, I'd been the first to race to the main house to get us food to eat together. Not only had I wanted to spend time with Zak, the truth was, in my naïve way, I'd wanted to take care of him too. And as a teenager, throwing together plates of food had been pretty much all I'd been able to manage.

"It's so good that you're home, son." After a wink, he headed past me. "I'll leave the veranda light on, and there's beer in the fridge," he called as he ventured closer to the house.

I smirked. "Thanks, Dad."

His hand lifted and he gave a small wave as he carried on walking. When he was firmly out of earshot, I faced the stable door and took a deep breath before I went inside.

I found him sitting on a small stool, beer in hand and looking directly at me. After the slightest of hesitations, I continued forward. While a part of me considered being a coward and hovering at the door, Zak deserved more than that. The closer I got, the more I struggled not to stumble. Still handsome, still built with a body I'd fantasised over countless nights, and still carrying that fierce gaze with his grey-green eyes that I was sure could see into my soul.

Around this guy, I'd always been the same— dreaming up descriptions on the cusp of damn poetry. Sometimes I wondered how I'd survived for so many years without him catching on to the depth of my feelings, and sometimes I wondered what it would have been like if I'd ever told him the truth.

Or certainly done so without me using my words as a weapon.

I shook the thoughts away. Yeah, he still affected me. I snorted internally as he continued to watch me in silence, while I'd stopped just a few short metres away. In truth, affected didn't even come close. A small, ridiculous part of me had hoped he'd look like shit and hadn't weathered well over the years. From what I saw of the man before me, he was travelling through his thirties somewhat spectacularly.

When his brow pitched high, I realised I'd been standing before him for Christ knew how long like a damn idiot. Awkwardness had charged into the room and ran around laughing its arse off at me. Not quite the way I'd planned for this to go, but it seemed fitting.

"Hey," I managed, my voice surprisingly steady. "So I have food for you." I held out the plate like an offering, hoping he'd do something beyond staring at me with his pretty eyes. When he remained silent, giving me absolutely nothing, I gnawed at the inside of my lip. I took a step forward and swung my gaze to the side where there was another small stool. "I'll just leave it here." Placing it down, I didn't dare risk a glance in his direction, especially considering our closeness.

Jesus, I hated this.

I could barely remember a time growing up without Zak being in the picture, and despite being so close to him, the closest I'd been in five years, I'd never felt further away. I straightened and took a step back. Aware I was going to make my mouth bleed with how damn hard I was worrying it, I needed to take action. To do that, I had to admit what a dick I'd been, and grovel—a lot.

With a sweep of my hand over my hair, I went ahead and blurted out the sorry that should have happened five years ago. "I fucked up." There was a slight flaring of his eyes. It wasn't a lot, but it was some sort of reaction at least. "I'm sorry. I shouldn't have…." I exhaled heavily, hating myself for being a coward and not doing this sooner. "I shouldn't have ever put you in that situation. I shouldn't have caused so much shit then run off."

My gaze followed his thumb as he brushed it across his lips a moment before he leaned forward, eyes still on me, and propped his elbows on his legs.

"And I should have called up straight away and tried to make it right, apologised." I cleared my throat, determined to not look away. "I'm sorry I screwed up and left like I did." I wanted to say I wished I could take it back, but that wouldn't have quite been the truth. I wanted to say I wished we could go back to being how we were, friends, but again, that was bullshit too. In the few moments I'd stood in front of him, I knew with absolute certainty that my feelings for the quiet cowboy in front of me hadn't changed. And being in love with a man who'd never so much as looked at me in a way beyond that of a big brother or mentor was a huge kick in the junk.

The silence was broken by a soft whinnying. I looked over in relief and saw the young mare, her stomach round and firm. "Is she okay?" I took the opportunity to change the subject, hoping he'd give me this. I pushed my hands in my pockets, still focusing on the pregnant mare. My hands tucked away, I no longer had to fear Zak seeing how shaken I was. I was humiliated enough as it was.

The stool creaked, and out of the corner of my eye, I saw Zak move. Keeping my body as relaxed as possible, I was aware of every step he took. When he finally stopped, he was by my side, looking in the direction of the horse he'd been caring for.

"She'll be okay." His nod was slight, but I still saw it. "And we'll get this figured out too."

When I angled my head in his direction, his gaze was already turned my way. "We will?" Was he really giving me this?

He tilted his head to the side, a casual move that

was familiar and sent a rush of heat to my stomach. "I still have it."

My eyes widened, understanding heating my cheeks. If there was ever a time for the earth to open up and select a victim, now would have been perfect. I wasn't that lucky. I shook my head. "Shit, I'm so so—"

"I know you are." He turned slightly and indicated I should follow him. I did so without question. He collected his plate of food, turned the large fans to a lower setting, and switched off the lights. We made our way towards his cottage, the bright moon guiding our way. Once there, he set his plate down on the outside table and headed towards the small building to the side, which he'd always used for projects.

The lights sprung to life a few moments after he hit the switch. Once my eyes adjusted, they jumped wide open as they landed on the machine off to the right. Still sleek, black, and sexy as hell stood his 1965 Royal Enfield. The biggest relief that sent shame thrumming through me was that it was intact. "How did you...?"

A grin stretched his mouth wide. "It took some doing. I was able to get a lot fixed, but a few parts took almost a year to track down to replace."

My eyes bounced between the bike I'd taken a bat

to the night I'd left town and the man before me. Why the hell he hadn't kicked my arse, I had no idea. I was grateful as hell. While I could hold my own at the gym and bench press a mean weight, his muscles were the product of hard work on the property, and there was no doubt in my mind he could put me to the ground.

"She's beautiful."

He nodded and looked my way. "She is that. Perfect, in fact."

I made a move to step closer but hesitated. I had zero right. This piece of engineering was more than a bike, and considering I'd set out to destroy it five years ago in a pathetic hissy fit of rage, it was a wonder he'd let me in the same damn room. Sickness churned my gut.

"You all right there?" he asked.

I nodded, not able to make eye contact in case I spewed.

"Shit, Leo, you've gone white as a damn ghost. You need to sit down or something?"

I snorted a humourless laugh. The apology was once again on the tip of my tongue, but I forced it away. Twisting my lips, I huffed out a breath through my nostrils. "Can I look at it properly?"

My eyes connected with his. As he slowly perused my features, a flicker of something appeared in his eyes. Before I could work out what exactly, he gave me a small nod. "Yep."

I hesitated a moment, waiting for a jab, a barb of sarcasm, a warning perhaps, but nothing came. I walked towards the bike, realising I should have known better. Zak had never been cruel, never used his words or his fists to unleash his disappointment or annoyance. Truth be told, all those years ago when I'd reacted, I'd done so not only in spite with jealousy spurring me on and my aching heart guiding me, but to egg him on, hoping for a reaction of some sort.

I closed my eyes, remembering the only reaction I received. A single look of abject disappointment. Running after that had been easy. It was a look that had hit me harder than any fist or cruel word.

"She looks incredible." The paint gleamed, even in the dull light coming from the bare overhead bulbs. "Does she start?"

Zak's heat was beside me a moment later. "She sure does. Not roadworthy yet, but not far off. We can start her tomorrow if you want, take her out on the concrete pad." His shoulder brushed mine, and I pressed my lips together, fighting my body's reaction to the touch and the proximity.

I had not returned home for this, to rekindle the crush I'd attempted to erase from my system over the past five years. Inwardly, I rolled my eyes at myself. I was 100 percent bullshitting myself. Something I noticed I was doing a lot in the few hours I'd been home. I'd never fully opened myself up to love again, not after years of loving the man by my side, and not after his painful rejection.

"You'd do that?" I didn't risk a glance at Zak as I reached out and stroked the tank. "You don't mind, not too busy?"

His deep voice was gruff and closer than I expected, making me jump. *Fuck.* "Not too busy when we've five years of catching up to do, Leo. You know me better than that."

I turned in his direction. My eyes widened when I discovered just how close he'd leaned in to speak to me. With my heart hammering in my chest, it was difficult to focus on anything beyond the feel of his warm breath brushing against my skin. Confusion battled the hit of lust racing through my veins and pooling in my gut. "I—" I attempted, but had to clear my damn throat as it threatened to close. "Yeah, I suppose I do."

His face gave nothing away as he stepped back. "Right, I best go eat before the possums get to it." Zak's lips quirked, and I smiled back in response.

"Yeah, okay, sure." Turning away from the bike, I willed myself to get it together. After all, Zak had given me a free pass. He hadn't made me grovel, nor had he brushed me aside. I was grateful, sure, but still, his forgiveness hummed of indifference, and damn if that didn't sting. The door creaked as he pushed it wide, allowing me to step into the still night. "I'll see what help Dad needs from me in the morning, and then we'll catch up." With forced casualness, I nodded and then walked away. "Night," I offered, waving my hand above my head as I made my way back to the main house.

"Night, Leo," trailed behind me. "Sleep well."

I quietly groaned. I doubted I'd be sleeping a wink until I left in a couple of weeks.

CHAPTER 4

Heat slammed down on me, hard and unforgiving. Lifting my Akubra, I welcomed the slight relief the stir of air provided. England had destroyed me. Hot days like these had been par for the course growing up, but five years of more grey skies than not had apparently destroyed my ability to survive and get on with the harsh demands of Australia. I swiped my brow and looked over at the large stables just a short walk away. Sod it. It had to be done.

I placed the fence ties and grips in the small bucket and stashed them next to one of the posts of the fence I was repairing. After making sure the bucket wouldn't topple, I started for the stables. There were two clouds in the sky, both far off in the distance and nowhere near the unrelenting sun. Like so many days, they'd offer no respite. But looking around my dad's farm, I was once again relieved to see so much welcome green grass. They'd had good rain at the beginning of summer, allowing for lush paddocks and full water tanks. It didn't mean anyone was able to relax, though. With autumn close by, there'd be dry spells and threats of drought on the horizon. But still, for the time being, everyone would be breathing a little easier.

As soon as my feet hit shade, I exhaled in relief. I removed my hat and placed it on the hook off to the right en route to the large barrel I hoped to God was still set up to the side. Seeing the full barrel, the water glistening and still, I grinned and unbuttoned the top two buttons of my shirt before pulling the damp material over my head. I set the shirt to the side and unceremoniously dunked my head in deep, allowing my neck to go under and my shoulders to touch the cool liquid.

My skin felt immediately refreshed, and I held my breath a few beats longer before coming up for air. Sweeping my dripping hair off my face, I cricked my neck from left to right. An appreciative groan escaped me when my vertebrae clicked and the tension eased a little. I needed to get my arse back into a farm-fit state, else there was no way I'd survive my time at home. I knew the only way to do so was to jump in and get my hands dirty. That and to make sure I used hot water when showering and took advantage of the ice machine my dad had.

A scuff of feet on the concrete floor had me angling towards the sound. My gaze landed on Zak, whose eyes were definitely not on my face. I quirked my brow, pretty damn sure his hard stare was on my arse. My pulse jumped at the prospect. Turning towards him, my gaze firmly on him, I watched amusedly when he jolted and his eyes lifted to mine. We stood facing each other, several metres between us, along with a new tension I had only experienced in my imagination.

"Ev—" The word came out with a croak. Actively avoiding acknowledging my heating skin, I cleared my throat and offered a small smile before saying, "Everything okay?"

His steady gaze roamed over my face, seeming to take every nuance in. The few seconds of silence stretched before finally, he nodded. His gruff voice sent a jolt of awareness through me when he answered, "Yeah, just checking up on you. Didn't see you, so was making sure you hadn't passed out from sunstroke or anything." His mouth twitched, and relief twirled in my gut.

I still knew him, even after all this time. Knew his quirks, his tells, knew that behind his quiet and at times curt exterior, there was often humour playing just below the surface. That lift of his lips right there meant he was taking the piss. Perhaps everything between us really could be okay, perhaps we could go back to how it had once been. Hope fought with frustration at the thought.

Pushing aside my disappointment, I latched on to the former emotion and snorted. "You saying I'm wet behind the ears or something?"

"Or something."

"Is that right?"

He shrugged, the action casual. But Zak never did anything without a purpose. Turning his head slightly to my right, his gaze left mine before he pointedly lifted one brow. I took the bait and followed his line of sight.

It was my saddle, looking well-oiled and not sporting a speck of dust. I swallowed hard, glancing between my favourite saddle and Zak. Had he really kept it cleaned and oiled to stop the leather from splitting, even after all these years? Breathing hard out of my nose, I took control of my emotions. I didn't even have to ask why he'd done it.

He was Zak.

It's what Zak always did. He always took care of me. Always. The knowledge had my heart punching against my ribcage.

"You think your arse can handle it?" With a

straight, even tone, he gave nothing, not until I burst out snickering, my emotion pushing the sound out louder than I intended. His laughter was like a balm over my needy soul. For five long years I'd been without it, and from just a few seconds of his deep laugh, I felt lighter, happier.

Fuck me dead. I finally felt home.

***

THE SUN DIPPED BEHIND THE DISTANT RANGE, AND I couldn't remember seeing a sunset quite as spectacular. While my backside genuinely hurt something rotten, and that was just after a couple of hours in the saddle, the sore arse cheeks and thighs were totally worth it. I glanced at Zak, whose eyes were fixed on the sunset. The slivers of sunlight left in the sky caught on the whiskers of his short beard.

Around a smirk, I asked, "Is that grey I see?"

He flicked his eyes to me, giving nothing away.

"Careful, you're going to blind me. It's glistening so damn much." I feigned a squint and chuckled.

"Glistening. Really?" This time he quirked his brow, giving me a little more of his focussed gaze.

"What?" I shrugged. "It's that fluff on your face that's doing all the glistening and shit, not mine." A shit-eating grin split my mouth wide.

Zak angled towards me. Jet, the horse he rode, shifted slightly at his movement. The stroke of his beard with his large hand held me captive. I was barely aware of his eyes roaming my face. "You know"—my eyes jumped from the movement to his eyes—"if I didn't know any better, I think there was envy in that comment of yours."

My heart picked up speed as the familiarity of his voice swept over me, along with the humour not many got the chance to see. "Is that right? You think there's a hint of green in my cheeks?"

His eyes zeroed in on my cheek closest to him for a moment, as if examining it. "In this light, there could quite possibly be. Fluff, my arse, boy."

A chuckle escaped me, filling the growing darkness around us.

Finally, he smiled. "You know, one day you may even be grown up enough to grow facial hair of your own. Maybe." His right brow rose in challenge.

"Hey," I said with a laugh. "I'm plenty grown and have to shave five times a day to keep on top of my manly beard that's always trying to escape." His guffaw rolled over me, relaxing my shoulders while making the long-forgotten wings take flight in my stomach.

He tilted his head and remained quiet a moment. I could no longer see his eyes properly, the dip of his hat and the sun obscuring them too much. "I can see that."

Frozen, I contemplated his words. Was he really saying what I thought… hoped he was saying? After a beat, and finally remembering to slam my gaping mouth shut, I hedged, "I missed you. This." My gulp was audible in the still evening. "I'm s—"

"Don't." He shook his head and lifted his Akubra off his head, revealing his eyes to me. "You've already apologised, and I've accepted." He twisted his mouth in thought, an expression he'd always done when mulling something over. "It was my fault as much as yours."

Confusion had my brows dipping. "I don't understand." And I really didn't. I'd been a wanker. I'd hit on him, which he'd rebuffed. It wasn't as if he'd been an arsehole about it. He'd been kind but firm. But he'd also known me too well, knew I would struggle with a no. I'd pushed him in the run-up to leaving for the UK and had made it pretty damn clear that I'd wait for him to be ready and I'd come back to him. The night before I'd left, I'd spotted him with one of the trainee ranch hands who'd been there for a spell. They'd been close, toe to toe, the guy's nose buried in Zak's neck.

After a bottle of Bundy rum, I'd lost my shit and behaved like the immature dick I had been.

I'd trashed his bike.

"Come on." He clicked at Jet, tightening the reins in his hands.

He was seriously not going to elaborate? Bewildered, I shook my head but held my reins firmly and followed suit. It wouldn't be long, maybe ten minutes before it was pitch-black. It was sensible to head back, but that didn't ease the confusion swirling in my mind.

The ride back was slow and silent, Zak watching the footing of his horse carefully. He knew every ridge, every hollow on this land. I had once. Aware we would carry on unspeaking, I considered how I could push Zak to explain himself. That I was surprised he'd admitted he was at fault, especially without further explanation, was an understatement. It was so unlike Zak. He never, and I meant *never* said or did anything without cause, without precision. Hell, sometimes I was convinced he put together a whole manual of cause and effect before acting on anything. So this was definitely something new. And I had no idea how I felt about that.

When we arrived at the stables, a noticeable tension rode the space between us. The air seemed thicker, charged. While loosening my neck, I reminded myself to breathe.

"Here."

My eyes latched on to Zak before travelling to his outstretched hand and the brush he held.

"Thanks." My fingers swept against his palm when I removed the brush. I glanced away quickly, focusing on my dad's horse and brushing her down. It was best I ignored the unfurling heat in my stomach. Plus those damn fluttering wings were back. This was dangerous, being so close to him, trying to make things like they had been. Too much had happened and changed.

I shook my head as I counted out my brush strokes, trying to use the monotony to soothe me. It was ridiculous. I clenched my jaw, frustration bubbling to the surface. I was a grown-arse man and needed to stop behaving like the brooding kid I'd left home as.

Screw it.

I turned abruptly, only to stumble, my eyes springing open so damn wide I was certain I looked like a damn cartoon character. Zak was before me. I would have been impressed with his ninja stealth skills had I not been so close to the guy.

His scent invaded my senses. Masculine, woodsy, and smelling a little like freshly cut hay. As I parted my mouth to ask what was going on, he took the words from me. His face lowered to mine, a move that was slow and deliberate. I had plenty of time to step back and stop the moment, but there was no chance of that happening. When his lips finally made contact with mine, I closed my eyes and edged closer to him. There wasn't a lick of space between us.

Our mouths fused. I groaned, our lips brushing together. Soft presses, scratches from his beard against my chin, and swipes of our tongues. There was nothing tentative about this kiss. It was heat, barely controlled desire I'd been managing to contain for ten years. With every brush of our lips, those damn wings took flight and I was sure they'd never settle ever again.

When his firm, rough hand clasped the back of my head, a low rumble sounded from the back of Zak's throat. God, the sound, the touch, the… everything… it was more than I'd ever imagined. The kiss slowed and I whimpered. Any other time I was sure humiliation would have followed from such a sound escaping, but screw that. This was Zak. He was going to pull away, and when he did, the word escaped unbidden. "No."

Zak leaned back enough so we could see each other clearly, but his hand remained, despite his fingers loosening a little in my hair. His eyes were dark, intense. "No?"

"Don't—" The word came out rougher than I intended. I blew a breath out of my nose and tried again. "Don't tell me it was a mistake." Honest to God, I wasn't beyond grovelling at this point. A flare of annoyance shot up my spine at the thought. Being vulnerable was shit. I detested it, and the way Zak affected me even after so much time apart pissed me off. It would have been easy to come back and not feel a damn thing, or even easier if he'd been with someone, but thi—

"I'm not."

Oh. His words were clear, his usual depth weaved through them. They also completely slammed the brakes on my internal struggle. He wasn't going to tell me it was a mistake. So did that mean…?

"So?" One-syllable words were my best way to navigate through this. My pounding heart made me breathless. If I tried for more, I was too afraid that damn whimper would slip out again.

Concern filled his eyes. Not surprising, since I was sure I was muttering riddles. Hell, I was the one who started this damn thing with a panicked *no*.

Knowing it was no good and that I couldn't rely on Zak to decrypt my wayward mumblings, I forced myself to take a breath and be coherent. "I thought you were going to push me away, say sorry, and—" I shrugged, a wry smile on my face. "—I don't know, walk away."

The grip he had on my head loosened to the point

of release, and he skimmed his fingers across my cheek. His mouth lifted into a small smile while he searched my eyes. "I wasn't. I was pulling away for a breath, to take a moment."

"Oh."

A small chuckle escaped his reddened lips. "Oh, indeed."

I shrugged again, my smile lifting and ease settling in my shoulders despite the tension still thrumming through my body. "So…" I leaned into his hand when his palm opened against my cheek. "Do you want to do it again? I'm okay with not taking a breath or a moment for as long as possible."

Zak's eyes lit with humour, and his grin was wide. "I'd like that, but shall we finish off the horses first and then head to my cabin? I have cold beer."

I didn't give a toss about beer at this point. I wanted another taste. Damn Zak and constantly being so pragmatic. I considered pouncing and fixing myself to him, his plan be damned, but Jet took that moment to whinny, drawing our attention his way. With a sigh, I hung my head. "I suppose we could do that." Defeat was in my voice, my tight jeans making it especially difficult to walk away. Not that I expected Zak to do anything about that tonight, but hell, if he offered, I'd have my zipper open so damn fast.

Rough fingers gripped my chin and tilted my head. His smile was the first thing I saw before my gaze landed on his sparkling eyes. God almighty, this guy was so freakin' handsome and perfect. "Come on." He planted his lips against mine. It was a simple peck but enough to have me groaning when he pulled away. He shook his head. "The sooner we get done here, the sooner we can chill."

My eyes widened. "Do you have Netflix?" My pulse galloped in my neck, and I cringed at my brain-to-mouth malfunction.

"Maybe," he answered wryly, and I was sure there was a twinkle in his eyes when he spoke.

It didn't take long to finish settling the horses and closing everything up for the night. Rather than heading straight to Zak's, I took a detour to the main house for a quick shower and to get changed. While sweat every now and then could be a turn-on in the right situation, I wanted to clean up. If I was lucky enough to get any action this evening, I wanted sweat-free balls. Just the thought of my freshly shaved goods in his mouth made said balls tighten. I groaned, trying to shake off the image before I headed to the kitchen to see what I could rustle up to take to Zak's.

"Where you off to?" Michelle's voice startled me

as I rummaged around in the fridge looking for left-overs before heading for my shower.

"Just looking for some tucker."

She walked to my side and got me to scoot over. "Heading on over to Zak's?" While she didn't look at me as she spoke, I still turned my head away. Heat full-on rushed my cheeks. "Yeah," I managed after clearing my throat.

"Uh-huh." Somehow she managed to make her response sound amused.

I flicked my gaze to her and raised a brow, looking for her to clarify.

Her wide grin was how she responded until I lifted both brows. "So this time are you making it stick?"

Surprise had me turning fully towards her. "Stick?" I legit had no idea what she was talking about.

"You and Zak." That was all she gave me as she lifted her own damn brows at me.

I shook my head and released a humourless huff. "Not sure stick is the right word." I winced immediately in embarrassment. "Don't even." I shook my head, my smile at odds with the heat licking against my cheeks. "What I meant was what are you talking about?" With no real clue why I was attempting to bullshit Michelle and play dumb, I lamely shrugged.

"Oh boy." The shake of her head was slow. "Sit your butt down, kiddo. Let's have a chat."

I didn't hold back my groan, but I did manage to dodge the clip around my ear she attempted. Laughing at my smooth moves, I focussed on that rather than whatever mortifying discussion she was going to have with me. It was like having the sex talk all over again.

"When you left, Zak took it the hardest."

I tensed, my heart starting to beat double time, the thud heavy and deafening.

"Every cent you've sent for us to give him to fix the mess you left, he refused."

My head jerked. "What?" Confusion coloured my question.

"Yep." Michelle nodded and sighed. "He refused every cent, saying it was unnecessary. Your dad put the money in your bank account and let him know it was there if he changed his mind. But you know Zak probably better than anyone. You know how damn stubborn he can be."

I really did. "Did he say why he wouldn't take the money?" Guilt renewed, I felt even shittier knowing he'd paid out to fix his bike himself. I'd sent a few thousand over the years, knowing fixing the machine wouldn't be cheap.

Michelle tipped her head to the side and offered

me a small smile. "Only that it was unnecessary and that it was his fault as much as yours."

Her words confused me as much as Zak's earlier ones had. Obviously, I had to have a conversation with the guy, as there was no way I could let this go. Not that I was looking to share the blame. I took full responsibility for not only my overreaction, but how ridiculous my behaviour had been.

While five years had passed by and I hoped like hell I'd grown wiser, it wasn't like I'd been a teenager when I acted out.

I released a heavy sigh. "Okay, thanks." The room went quiet, my thoughts unsettled.

"Listen." Michelle reached out to me and patted my forearm. "Just go and shower up. I'll sort you guys some food, and just enjoy your time while you're at home, okay?"

I nodded and offered her a tired smile. "Yeah, sounds good. Thanks." I stood and placed a kiss on her head, then made my way to the shower.

While the taste of Zak was still on my lips, my libido had fizzled away. I groaned in frustration as the hot water pounded against my bare skin. The heat felt good, but my plans for making out with Zak didn't seem such a great idea anymore. Okay, not quite true. Hell, he was so damn hot, and that kiss… it was better than any and every fantasy I'd ever had.

The thought of more—I groaned again. The thought of more was actually dangerous.

In less than a fortnight I'd be heading back to the UK, where I had a flat, friends, a career. If I started anything with Zak now, I didn't know if I could ever come back from that.

That didn't stop me wondering about the what-ifs though.

CHAPTER 5

A restless sleep followed. For most of the night, I lay awake thinking of Zak, his kiss, and his determination to shoulder some of the blame. Last night had not gone as planned at all. Certainly not what I'd envisioned after the mind-blowing kiss we'd shared.

I'd gone over with just his food and then walked away with a tentative smile. It was a dick move, and I still wasn't quite sure why the hell I'd left. And to be honest, how I'd managed it after what we'd shared in the barn.

It was no good. I threw back my covers, switched on my light, and made my way to the kitchen. Coffee was definitely in order. I'd need it to get through the day, especially with the fencing I'd promised my dad I'd carry on helping Zak replace.

It was only 5:00 a.m., so I had an hour before Zak

was expecting me. It gave me time to inhale caffeine and also get ready for the day. There was so much left unsaid between Zak and me. Yeah, there was that bloody amazing kiss, but I couldn't ignore the worry churning inside.

Any other guy, I'd not concern myself with the possibility of getting my dick wet, but this was Zak. He would never be a man I could hook up with and walk away from. With so much history, it would be impossible.

With just ten minutes to go before Zak was expecting me, I was jittery with nerves. The opening of the kitchen door had my head jerking in its direction.

Zak.

Our eyes connected. Trying to act nonchalant was pointless. All coolness disappeared as heat rushed to my cheeks and my pulse rate increased. Zak's smile reached his eyes as he strode fully into the room and closed the door behind him. With his gaze locked on to mine, he moved towards me while I remained rooted to the spot.

I hesitated, considering stepping towards him. Hell, a greeting perhaps would have helped too, but breaking free from the intensity of his gaze proved impossible. He raised one eyebrow and was in my space a mere moment later.

His work-roughened hand brushed my cheek as he gently held the back of my neck. I swallowed hard at the contact of his skin against mine, at the fact that everything that had happened yesterday was real.

He pulled me closer, his thigh touching mine. He peered down into my eyes and tilted my chin slightly. Was he going to kiss me? I was totally down for some lip action, despite being in my folks' kitchen and knowing they could walk in at any minute. But Zak knew that too, so I was curious what his next move would be. Regardless of the analysis going on inside my head, I held my breath, desperately wanting his lips on mine, knowing it would be even better than yesterday. There was a moment's hesitation, his eyes searching mine as a slight frown sat on his face. It remained there a fraction of a second, but I saw it. I felt his confusion, his debate, and I wondered if he was thinking about what all this really meant for the two of us.

The seconds felt more like minutes as the room around me blurred, my focus only on him. Finally, his lips brushed mine for just a moment. As quickly as it happened, he released my face and took my hand, leading me out of the house.

I allowed myself to be led—as if I had any choice. All rational thought had dissolved, even before the kiss, but the barest of kisses left my head spinning. So follow him I did.

Once in the cooler morning air, my lust-fogged brain cleared just slightly. That was, until Zak backed me against the side of the house.

My stomach tightened, my breathing increasing. This was a side of Zak I'd never seen before.

"Morning." The deep rumble of his voice had me flipping my gaze to his before it dropped to his mouth, which was now sporting a small smile.

"Morning." My voice was gravelly, coming out deeper than usual. "Everything okay?" Once more, my eyes searched his.

Zak gave the briefest of nods before he brushed a tender kiss to my lips. My eyes fluttered closed, despite wanting to take him and his movements in. This guy unravelled me and made my damn head spin. While he always had, my crush alone was nothing compared to the real thing of his heat pressed against me.

When he pulled away, I snapped my lids open.

"Yeah. Kind of figured since I didn't kiss you last night after you dropped off the food, I should just do so now."

I raised a brow, desire and confusion at war. I opened my mouth to speak, but then paused and slammed my mouth shut, not quite sure how to really begin to make sense of this massive change.

"What?" He edged back a little, as if giving me room to breathe. I needed it, but that didn't stop me from reaching out to him and settling my palm on his waist. His shoulders appeared to relax a little at my touch. "What were you going to say?"

Honesty. Yeah, so bloody easy in principle to follow the set pattern and belief that we'd always try to be honest with each other. That didn't quite work out for me in the past when he swept aside my advances and disputed my feelings. After yesterday though, things had changed. I owed it to both of us to clear the air.

"I just...." I wrinkled my forehead, searching for the right words. "What's changed? Why now?"

He didn't sigh like I'd half expected him to. Instead, he took hold of my hand and urged me to follow him. "I'd hoped we could have talked last night," he threw over his shoulder. Not quite reproachful, but there was a hint of something in his tone. But tough shit. I couldn't have dealt with it last night.

"It would have been too easy," I admitted.

He cast a quick glance over my shoulder, quirking his brow in question as he led us towards his place.

"Coming over, staying, finishing what I desperately wanted in the barn." A small shrug lifted both of my shoulders as we stepped up on to his veranda, and he released my hand as he took a seat on one of the benches there. "I can't just fall into bed and fuck. Not with you." I ignored the heat touching my cheeks. It was too important to get this all said.

Zak's eyes widened for the barest of moments before he seemed to school his features. A move I was used to. "We'd never just fuck." His gaze was steady, his voice clear, and holy crapping hell, my groin tightened when he said "fuck."

A bubble of laughter burst free from my tense body. "Dude. You know that's the first time I've ever heard you say fuck." I laughed harder, my tension rolling away. Zak was the epitome of responsible, and while he had moments of cussing, he'd always reined himself in. With my forearms pressing against my thighs, my back bent forward, I turned my head towards him, a big-arse grin on my face. "I just don't know what to think."

He mirrored my position, putting our faces close in the process. "About what exactly?" While there was humour alight in his gaze, the crinkles around his eyes more pronounced, the rest of his features didn't give me any insight into his thoughts.

"You," I admitted. "You're still the same but you're now, what? Flirting with me, swearing—"

"Kissing you."

My eyes sprang open so damn wide I was in danger of them popping out of my head. "Yes, *that*, and you even saying that." I shook my head, pulling my gaze from him and looking out at the stables. "You knew how I felt before I left… for years," I clarified, my gaze still averted, "yet now I come back, on holiday I will add, and you're doing this now." I blew out my cheeks, no real idea where I was going with any of this.

His thigh brushed against mine as he manoeuvred a little. "You don't want me to say or do those things." There was a beat of silence before I realised he'd made a statement rather than asking me to clarify. "Leo, I'm sorry. I thought—" He broke himself off and cleared his throat. The action had me snapping my head to his.

When he stood abruptly, a strange smile on his face, one I was pretty damn sure was not real, I sat up.

"So, I'm sorry," he said again. "I can keep working by myself today if you want. I understand if—"

"For real." I shook my head, bemused. "Of course I want you to do and say those things. Shit… so damn much." I stood and positioned myself before him. Zak's eyes roamed my face, and for quite possibly the first time ever, a hint of pink spread across his cheeks. My heart raced, the sensation of affecting him so much heady.

"You do?" He tilted his head, his voice uncertain.

I wanted to laugh, to snort, but I wasn't quite sure he'd appreciate it. Not about this. Pressing my lips together, I stepped directly into his space and looped my arms around his waist, shoving my hands in his back pockets. "So much so, my mind is spinning," I said honestly. "I just need to understand, is all. And I need to get my head around what this means."

He relaxed and wrapped his arms around me, pulling me towards him. Rather than a kiss, he hugged me tightly. "Yeah, I can see you need to know that." He chortled, the sound and movement rocking us both. The laugh was warm and welcoming and had my lips lifting into a smile. "Yesterday I kinda changed things, huh?"

This time I snorted against his chest and squeezed against him a little tighter. "You think?" I angled away. "So we need to talk without me just going ahead and jumping your bones." His face lit with amusement as I continued. "That was one of the main reasons I legged it yesterday after dropping off the food for you. Any indication you'd be dropping your pants, and you wouldn't be able to blink before I'd be on my knees."

Zak's wide eyes and slack jaw was the best thing ever. I'd matured a lot since being away—well, in some ways. It seemed he wasn't quite as prepared for that as maybe he'd thought.

After slamming his mouth shut, he cleared his throat and laughed. "Okay then. That's... fair enough." He shrugged and gave me a smile.

I grinned back at him, enjoying the changes in our relationship and loving once more the heat in his cheeks. I hoped to God he was imagining me on my knees. Biting the inside of my cheeks to control the humour that was on the verge of inappropriate hysterics, I squeezed his butt cheeks once and then stepped out of his hold.

"Okay," I said with a nod. "Fencing and then dinner and talking, with no being on my knees and getting distracted." I spun on my heels before he could respond, no longer feeling quite at odds as I had when I'd first woken up.

"So maybe it *was* me."

Zak's snort was more like a grunt. "No shit." I looked across at him and watched him shake his head. "Your head visible above the bush was a dead giveaway." He threw me a lopsided grin. "It was cute, though." A sexy wink followed.

I shot him the stink eye, but he just laughed harder. "I can't believe you've known all this time." Embarrassment shot through me. "I'd been sure I was stealthy."

"Ha!" He stood up straight and stretched his back. "Nope. You were louder than a bloody kookaburra in mating season."

I shook my head, no idea if kookaburras were louder in season or not, but still. "But you chose to ignore it," I challenged.

With one arm propped on the fence post, he looked the epitome of a red-hot cowboy who I couldn't wait to sink my teeth into. "What was I supposed to do? Call out a seventeen-year-old jerking off to me swimming in the dam." He rolled his eyes.

Change that to arsehole cowboy. "Well." I shrugged, aware he'd sort of made a good point. "You could have given me the nod or something. Maybe it would have stopped me from being caught by Michelle behind the barn a couple of weeks later."

His laugh was loud and abrupt. "Was that what you were doing that time I was changing the discs?"

"Trying to or about to. Michelle caught me with my hands down my pants. Literally. Told her I'd been bitten by a mozzie and was itchy as hell." I grinned at the memory while Zak all but wheezed, tears leaking out of his eyes. "Do you not realise how freakin' hot you looked, shirt off, oiled skin...." I shivered in delight at the memory and then paused abruptly before tilting my head, eyes narrowing. "Why weren't you wearing a shirt?"

The wheezing laughter cut off abruptly and he straightened, clearing his throat. "I'd spilt oil," he said after a few beats. "The damn stuff was everywhere."

"Bullshit." I grinned wide, realizing he was totally full of it. "Why?"

Hand to the back of his neck, he huffed out a breath. "I can't believe I'm admitting this." My mouth stretched wide, waiting for him to continue. "I may have known you were there and spying on me."

My mouth dropped wide and my brows shot high. "Are you for real?"

He shrugged while my heart hammered, not quite sure what to do with this information. "Maybe," he admitted, looking decidedly shifty. "What?"

If my mixed feelings were showing on my face, it was no wonder he was asking. "But—" I slammed my mouth shut. "Why?" Did that mean he'd seen me, as in really *seen* me back then?

In three strides he was before me. "Do you not

remember the seventeen-year-old you?" He shook his head. While his eyes were on mine, he seemed adrift in memory. "Christ, Leo, you were bloody jail-bait waiting to happen."

Eyes wide, I stood before him, somehow remembering to breathe. "So you thought I was hot?" I'd meant for my words to come out light and teasing. Instead, they came out bewildered.

"Hot doesn't come close to how gorgeous you were. Are." A chagrined smile lifted his lips.

While the knowledge did a whole heap to my ego, questions flittered through immediately. I pursed my lips in consideration. "So why—" Zak's sigh stopped me in my tracks. "What?"

With a swipe of his finger against my cheek, his gaze roamed my face. "I just know what you're going to say, to ask, and it all comes down to what happened when you left after uni to head to the UK."

He was right. With a simple nod, I confirmed it.

"Listen, I'm not deliberately stalling." My wide eyes challenged that. A soft smile was his response, with a small shake of his head. "Honestly, I'm not. I just don't think it's a conversation we should be having here, now, sweaty, hot, and hungry."

Heat flared in my body and I grinned. "You know, we can fix all three of those things at once." Despite my smile still firmly in place and the lightness in my voice, I was dead set serious.

He groaned and tilted his head back to the clear blue sky. "You're really not helping," he said, his face lowering once again.

"I can help," I offered salaciously, this time with my brows wiggling. "But I do understand why perhaps now isn't the best time to chat. I suppose. I will add that I say so reluctantly."

"I know." He nodded. "And I'm sorry. It's not like I'm deliberately building this into a big deal or anything." He finished his words with the barest of kisses against my lips.

He spoke the truth. One of the many amazing things about Zak was that he didn't indulge in drama, so I'd give him this out.

"Shall we grab lunch now?" he asked as he took a step away.

"Sounds good."

"Come on then." We headed to the ATV after picking up some of the fencing equipment we didn't want left around, and drove to the smaller barn in the large paddock we were in. We were a fair distance from the house, and this was the closest shade.

Once there, Zak opened the Esky, producing sandwiches and cold water. I accepted them gratefully and started munching. We ate in companionable silence for a while. After washing the food down with the water, I leaned back against the packed bales of hay to the side. "You got any trainees coming out later in the year?" While I was genuinely interested in the answer, to know what was going on, the mention of trainees had my stomach dipping and Zak's eyes hardening a little.

"No." He shook his head, then seemed to take his time to open the cap on his bottle and have a swig.

"How come?" My brow creased. My dad's place was a hotbed for trainees. Who wouldn't want a placement at such a prominent stud farm?

Silent for a beat, then two, Zak finally cleared his throat. "Jason's not going to be around to help train this year, and obviously your dad can't take on anyone...." He seemed to trail off, punctuating his words with a careless shrug.

Confused, I asked, "But... isn't that your gig?" For at least four years when I'd still been in Australia, Zak had taken on trainees. His patience was perfect for the job. I could understand why Jason, a great guy who worked for Dad, would also work with them, but him not being around meaning no trainees made no sense.

Zak's voice came out flat. "Not anymore."

My heart rate legit spiked as I tried to make sense

of everything. Needing to know, I asked, "When was the last time you took on a trainee?"

"There were a couple here last year."

"No." I was already shaking my head. "You?"

I watched, transfixed, as his tongue pushed his cheek out before he bit the side of his lip and finally huffed out a breath. "So we're doing this now and not waiting, huh?"

I shrugged. "I hadn't realised that's what we were doing when I asked," I admitted, barely hearing my words due to the pounding of my heart.

"Darren was the last trainee I took on." His gaze locked on mine as he spoke, and I just knew he was waiting for my reaction. But I had zero idea what I was going to do with that information.

I nodded, trying to figure out exactly how the knowledge made me feel. "Okay." I coughed to clear my throat. "Not sure what to ask or say, to be honest." I did not want to behave like a jealous dick. Darren had been the cum stain who'd had his tongue shoved down Zak's throat the night before I'd left. Darren had been twenty-frickin'-two. It didn't take a genius to figure out why I'd overreacted and kicked off to the point of ridiculousness. While I'd been hurt, which was a massive understatement, there was no doubt my trashing his bike was unforgiveable and just downright pathetic. But still, it had happened.

That still led me to the warring information coming to light.

Zak had thought my seventeen-year-old self was hot. So I could only assume my twenty-two-year-old self had been just as hot, if not even hotter. I'd worked hard to perfect my labour-hardened muscles back in the day.

Zak had also known I was very actively lusting after him.

I was also pretty sure Zak knew my feelings, what, seven years or so in the making back then, were a damn lot stronger than simple lust. I'd all but told him before I left.

So that led me back to the *why* of it all. Why Darren and not me? And why did that question pop into my head like a whiney bloody lovesick dickhead? I seriously couldn't win.

"You want to know why, right?"

Relief had me nodding. I sounded like a dick in my own mind, so that he prevented me from showing just how pathetic I could be was a boon. "Just a little." A small scoff followed my words.

"Are you happy in England?"

Surprise had me doing a double take. *Huh?* "What?" Here I was waiting for answers from my misspent youth, and he was throwing me off the trail with random questions.

"Are you happy in England? In your job? Where you live? With your… friends?"

"Yeah, I suppose. I get up, go to work, get shit done. Hang out." I shrugged. "I've already told you about the trips I take." During the countless conversations we'd had over the last week.

"You suppose?" Unwavering eyes met mine.

"Erm… yeah?" The question was there, uncertain of his point.

Gaze still hard, he didn't back down as he said, "What does that even mean?"

I frowned. "You know, perhaps if you just asked what you really wanted to know I could catch up."

"I thought my question was fairly straight-forward."

Okay, admittedly it was. "I suppose, but what I'm getting at is the why of it all." My eyes sprang open as soon as I stopped talking. "You want to know if I'm coming home."

Zak's shoulders visibly relaxed as he nodded. "Yeah."

Hell, emotion slammed into me, tickling my nose. Bloody thing. Unable to take the distance, considering what we were talking about, I stood and walked over to him, taking a seat next to him but angling so I could see his face. Focussing hard at keeping my emotions in check, I asked, "Do you want me home?"

"I miss you. I've always wanted you at home, but it's important that you make your own choices. Decide what makes you happy." His hand reached out and clasped mine. "Five years ago, I didn't want to pressure you."

"And you do now?" A smile curled my lips as I squeezed his hand. He gave me a deadpan look, and I laughed. "What? Okay, you know that I'm joking, well, sort of." I tugged his hand up so I could press my lips against his weathered skin. "I miss home, miss Dad, Michelle, and my sister." I pressed my lips to his mouth. When I pulled away, I whispered, "I missed you." I edged further away to avoiding kissing him again. "Coming home to the sunshine wouldn't be the worst thing ever. I just need to know if coming home means I'll be coming home to you too. That after all this time, all this waiting, we can make a go of it."

Certainty filled every word I spoke. There was no second-guessing, no doubt. Above all else, I was sure that there could truly be a future with Zak. Truth be told, I didn't give a shit about the lost time, the hurt. To amalgamate and have the time to figure out us as a couple was worth the growing up I'd needed to do.

"I'd really like that." His smile reached his eyes.

"Yeah?"

He nodded. "More than anything."

My lips were on his an instant later. Hot and heavy, they were perfect. Zak's strong arms wrapped around me and he tugged me over so I was flush against him and on his lap straddling his thighs. When his fingers traced my cheekbone, he angled himself away. "I'm sorry for letting him kiss me when I knew you were watching."

"Seriously, Zak, there's a thing called timing. Me, hot and needy on your lap is no such time."

He gripped my arse cheek with the one hand that wasn't touching my face. "Maybe. But I'm just too old to not lay it all out there. I did it. Let him kiss me. Yeah, there was no doubt a better way of handling it, but it's done, and I'm sorry."

While the truth of what had happened hurt, five years had whizzed on by. "Well, you are getting old, so— Ouch." He squeezed my butt hard. "I'm just agreeing with what you said. Geez, man."

His lips twisted, and I couldn't resist pressing my lips back to them.

"Oh… so, erm…." An awkward cough followed, and I froze. Still pressed against Zak's lips, my eyes sprang open to see Zak's own staring back at me.

Busted.

I pulled back, eased off Zak, not so subtly pulling

my shirt out of my jeans before I stood and turned. My dad seeing my boner was not on my list of things to achieve today, or ever. "Hey, Dad." I gave an awkward wave, and immediately shot Zak the stink eye as he guffawed while standing. He proceeded to shake his head at my ridiculous hand that was still weirdly in the air. I turned my gaze back to Dad just as Zak stood by my side and clasped my hand.

Wide-eyed, I almost gave myself whiplash as I jerked my head to look at Zak, before focussing on my hands, back to Dad, then to Zak. "For real?" My whisper wasn't quite low. It sounded edgy. It wasn't like my dad hadn't seen me holding hands with a guy before—admittedly only a couple of times—but still, this was Zak.

Zak's response was to smile broadly and squeeze my hand.

Alrighty then. I turned my attention back to my dad, my heart melting at Zak's gesture. Without a doubt, we were doing this.

When my eyes connected with my dad's, I stilled. "Dad," my voice was higher pitched than normal, alarm heightening it, "are you... are those tears?" What the frick was happening? The world was turning on its head.

My dad quickly shook his head and cleared his throat one too many times. "No." He followed up with a tut, indicating I was being ridiculous. "Just the bloody dust in this damn place. Damn antihistamines aren't working again."

Zak tensed beside me, and I was sure he was holding back his snort. Me, however: "Yeah, right. You don't have allergies, old man. What gives?"

His voice, still gruff from the emotion that was apparently dust, filled the small barn. "I just needed Zak's help with Phillipa. Can you bear to be without him for that long?" He quirked his brow at me, and I was damned if that bloody dust hadn't got into my own eye. My dad was a dead-set legend.

"He's all yours for the afternoon, as long as he's mine for the rest of the time." My dad was a straight shooter. It was best to simply say it how it was. He wasn't one to read between the lines.

"Is that right?" He shot his gaze to Zak. "So you convinced him, huh?"

What the— "You knew…." Unsure how to finish that, I gestured wildly in the air. Again. Zak, angling away from my flying hand, tugged me closer and wrapped an arm around me. He was smiling at me when I looked at him. This guy was going to turn me into mush before the day was done.

"That the old fart wanted to finally talk you into being his beau."

I quirked my brow at that. "Beau? Really, Dad?"

He shrugged. "Whatever, son, but yeah."

I grinned at my dad, kinda loving that he and Zak were in cahoots. I had no idea when that had happened or how it had happened, and while I was keen to know, I was all about the present.

"Does the 'rest of the time' mean you're finally leaving Pommy land and coming home?"

With a quick glance at Zak, I turned my focus back to Dad. "Yeah. Figured it was time to sort this half-arsed joint of yours out. Plus, you know, there's seeing you guys. And Jen pretty much said she'd disown me if I was away much longer." I bumped into Zak a little as I said, "Plus there's Zak here, who apparently can't resist me or cope without my awesome self in his life."

I laughed loudly when Zak dug his fingers into my ribs and broke away. I threw him a wink before heading to my dad. Once before him, I smiled. "It's time to come home."

Clasping me around the back of my head, my dad tugged me into his arms and hugged me hard. "Good to hear it, son." He pressed a brief kiss to my temple before stepping away. "I'll tell Michelle we're cele-brating and to give Jenny a call." I nodded, liking the sound of that. "Zak, ready?"

"Sure thing." He passed me by and threw me a

wink. "The keys are in the ATV," he said. "I'll see you at dinner."

I nodded, a little dumbly truth be told. It seemed there was a whole heap of changes afoot that I needed to get figured out quick smart.

CHAPTER 6

The day was a grueller. While I'd been more than happy to lend a hand and flex some unworked muscle over the past week or so, I'd foolishly forgotten just how demanding life on the property could be. Didn't mean I wasn't enjoying it. Far from it, in fact.

I'd managed to have a heap of time with my family, and some much-needed one-on-one time with my sister after she'd nagged me for brother-sister time.

Plus, while I'd be focussed on the business side of things when I came home, there was no doubt I'd be spending time doing manual labour on the farm too. After the past couple of weeks of fencing, fixing up one of the smaller stables, and riding, every muscle and bone in my body had been worked over.

Zak thought my pain was hilarious. Bastard.

"Here." I turned just as a small bale of hay hit me in the chest. I grunted and wrapped my arms around it.

"Bloody hilarious."

His laughter suggested he thought it was.

It had been like this since we'd shared our first hot kiss. Laughter, stolen kisses, and a natural ease that had never truly disappeared.

"What?" he asked, far too innocently. "Not my fault you're moping around."

Moping? I was flippin' knackered. Not only was I doing all I could on the farm, admittedly so I could spend time with Zak, I'd been spending hours sorting out my move back to Australia.

I flipped him off and searched around for something to throw at him. But he shook his head at me just as I spotted the small bucket of water sitting off to the side.

"Don't even think about it."

"You know," I raised my brows in challenge, "that just makes me want to do it all the more."

"I'm not too old to kick your arse, you know."

I grinned. "Just old enough, huh?"

He threw me a deadpan look. "I age like good whiskey."

A snort escaped immediately. "Seriously, you

want to stick with that comparison? How about chees
—" I grunted again as he threw another small bale at
me. This time I landed on my arse. His laughter
reached my ears just as his hand appeared to help me
up. I grinned and gripped his glove-covered palm,
allowing him to tug me up.

Once on my feet, I shook my head. "You know,
it's a good job you're hot, else I'd be all levels of
pissed off."

He grinned as he stepped into my space, my hand
still in his. "Hot, huh?"

I rolled my eyes. "Please."

This time his brows bouncing up and down made
it impossible to keep my own smirk off my face.
"You're an idiot."

"Your idiot."

My eyes connected with his. "Yeah?"

He nodded, his gaze intent. "Always."

Longing struck me hard. The kisses and the time
we'd spent together were phenomenal, more than I'd
ever imagined. My decision to come home had been
easy. "You know, Michelle spoke to me about you
when I first came home."

"She did?" He looked surprised.

"Yeah." I reached out and swept my thumb over
his cheek, loving the familiarity of his rough skin.
"She asked when I was going to make it stick." His

eyes darted between my eyes and my lips as I spoke. "I was a little thrown when she said that. Not quite sure how it could happen," I admitted.

Zak moved an inch closer, angling his face down a little, his warm breath making the hairs on my arms stand to attention.

"Do you know how it could happen?" His voice was conspiring, almost at a whisper.

I swallowed hard at the intensity in his gaze, the longing I thought I saw there. "I—"

A shrill cry of pain had Zak whipping around and me gasping.

Shit.

I WOULD NOT PUKE. NO WAY. NUH-UH.

It had to be superficial, but Jesus, there was a lot of blood. When I'd mentioned that to Zak, the idiot had just said he was relieved it was his and not Phillipa's, the damn clumsy horse that she was. Somehow, she'd got herself caught in a jumble of barbed wire, which had set Zak off on a rant that I would have found hilarious if it hadn't been for the fact that in helping her, he'd managed to get himself in a fight with the wire.

He'd lost.

Once inside Zak's place, he directed me to his bedroom. The number of times over the last week I'd fantasised about being in his room and finally having the chance to strip him down brought heat to my cheeks. It was only Zak wincing in pain when trying to remove his torn jeans that refocused my attention.

"Let me help you." Gently removing his boots, I allowed my eyes to linger on his strong, jean-clad thighs. As he unbuttoned his jeans, I hesitated, unsure of what support to offer. Flustered, my voice came out slightly high-pitched. "Err, can I help?"

Zak faced me, taking in my flushed cheeks. He arched an eyebrow and barely spoke above a whisper. "Maybe you should sit this one out. I might forget about my injury if you remain down on your knees in front of me."

His words took a moment to sink in. "Oh. Oh, in that case, I'll sit over here." I stood and stepped back. I hesitated before sitting at the edge of his bed, wishing there was a chair to sit on instead. I attempted to avert my eyes as Zak peeled off his jeans and revealed muscular legs with dark hair. Of course I totally watched him. My pretence at giving him privacy was a farce. Keeping my mind out of the gutter and away from him being in his underwear, I swept my gaze around the room. His bedroom hadn't changed from the first time I'd snuck into here when I was a teenager and I'd been snooping. Solid drawers, a couple of bedside tables, and a small closet filled the space, and a door to his en suite bathroom was situated to the right.

Sensing Zak's stillness, I glanced back at him. I stood swiftly and advanced to his side. "Your thigh." I winced. It didn't look deep enough for stitches, but it looked sore as hell. "It seems like the bleeding has stopped, but we need to get it cleaned up." I glanced in the direction of his bathroom. "Do you have a first aid kit, or should I grab one from the main house?"

Zak smiled, easing himself on to the bed and pointing at the bathroom door, a wide grin on his face. "In there."

My mouth twisted before I made to move. "Any reason you're grinning?"

He shrugged, the smile still plastered on his face. "Just never figured you for the nurse type."

I flipped him off and headed to the bathroom. "You'll see exactly how nurse-like I can be in a minute, arsehole." His laughter followed my words.

It didn't take me long to find cotton wool, a small first aid kit, and a bowl, which I filled with warm water. Zak smiled when he saw my supplies. "Playing nurse suits you." He wriggled his brows in my direction, and for a moment, I considered dumping water in his lap.

I rolled my eyes and cleaned his wound. With all the blood removed, the damage was really very little. Thank Christ. Gauze and tape would do the trick.

"Is it too tight?" I asked when I noticed a pained look on his face. Maybe I'd stretched out the tape and caught his skin or something. Between his legs, I was leaning over him. "I just don't want the bleeding to start again."

"Leo." Zak reached up and held my wrist gently. He closed his eyes for a moment before peering back up at me. His eyes widened as if trying to get me to understand the words he wasn't saying.

I went to step back, but Zak's hand tightened on my wrist, preventing me. He pulled me closer to him. This time I was viscerally aware of my position and just how damn close I was to him.

I made to speak when he stood and wrapped his arms around my waist. His hand pressed against my back, forcing me even closer to his firm body.

"I don't thin—"

His lips stopped all words and thought.

Effortlessly, he changed our positions and urged me onto the bed. I went willingly.

He stood above me, eyes raking over my body. Before I had time to react, let alone beg him to hurry the hell up, he leaned towards me, his hands going straight to my belt.

Hell yes, this I could get on board with.

His cool fingers brushed the exposed skin above my jeans. Impatient, desperate to get a look, a touch, hell, a taste of him, I returned the gesture by reaching out to the band of his boxer briefs and easing them down, remembering to be careful around his injury.

Zak, exposed in all of his true, hard glory, was perfect. He groaned in response as I wrapped my hand around him. Before my mouth could travel the path of my hand, he kissed me again. There was urgency in his touch, reaching a level of intensity verging on desperation. His work-roughened hands brushed across my chest. With a huff, he yanked off my shirt. His quickly followed. Next, his fingers landed on my nipple. I groaned. My nipples were tender as hell when I was turned on, and considering I was fit to explode, I couldn't do anything but arch closer to him and gasp.

"Zak." The word was ragged and filled with need. His smile pressed against my lips between his kisses as his hand traced the contours of my stomach. How the hell could he be smiling when in pain? Seriously, anytime now I'd explode. Fuck. His fingers reached for my open jeans before he angled away and tugged them down.

Both of us bare-arsed naked was something to behold, a moment I'd fantasized and jacked off to too many times, and years, to count. His palm reached me, gently caressing and stroking. I gripped his length and moved my hand quickly.

"This is how we make it stick."

My eyes widened at his declaration, and I found myself nodding immediately.

"That, and maybe the fact that I fell so damn hard years ago."

Words I'd only dreamed he'd utter were finally in the air. There was nothing left between us.

He leaned over and pressed his lips to mine, this time softer. When he pulled away, he cupped my cheek. "You top, right?"

I nodded. "Yeah, but I can bottom too."

His eyes turned molten. "This time. Next, I want you to take me."

I was totally down for that.

I scooted back on the bed as Zak made his way to his bedside table. "I know you're on PrEP, right. I wasn't sure—"

I looked at the condom as well as the lube in his hand. "I'd like to go without. I know for damn sure I'm not positive for anything other than blue balls."

His laughter was deep and infectious. "Yeah, I think that's quite possibly the only thing I'm registering positive for as well."

He settled on the bed next to me, and I sat up,

needing his lips on mine. Satisfied with the deep kiss and the increasingly ragged breaths coming from the both of us, I took the bottle from him.

"Let me." His hand on the bottle stopped me, and I settled back happily.

A loud groan rent the air. Mine. Zak was a freaking tease. He was going to kill me before he finally managed to plant himself balls deep at this rate. I heard myself chanting nonsensical words as he entered another digit. I had no idea how many that was. He was slow at first, but I needed more. Finally needed him deep inside me. I grasped hold of his arm and shook my head.

"I can't, I just need."

Satisfaction painted his features as he edged away and repositioned himself. A trickle of cool lubricant had me gasping once more. I pulled him towards me, allowing him to fill me completely after a few carefully timed moments. Rightness settled through me. The fullness perfect. With his lips finding mine, we built up speed.

"Just…" More gobbledygook spurted from my mouth. The only word coming out clear was "More."

We pushed harder and deeper as the heat of my release spread through my body. The soles of my feet pressed hard into the mattress as he worked in a perfect rhythm. Stars exploded, my toes curled painfully, and I wasn't quite sure if I'd ever be able to see straight again. Let alone walk.

Our bodies shook as a breathless Zak bent down for another kiss. "Can I be cliché?"

I grinned, sure my smile was lopsided. My half-mast eyes peered up at him, and I groaned as he moved slightly. "Go for it," I all but mumbled, sleep beckoning in sated bliss.

"Us making it stick means I love you. You know that, right?"

After a brief nod, I angled up, silently asking for a kiss. His lips found mine, warm and oh so sweet. Pressing my head against the pillow, I focussed on his words, focussed on my heart beating for this gorgeous man who'd had my love seemingly forever.

"I know," I answered sleepily. "I love you too."

I HOPE THIS SHORT, LOW-ANGST READ OFFERED YOU THAT little escapism for a couple of hours. It was such fun to write.

If you're looking for more Aussie heat and sweetness, check out NOT USED TO CUTE. I think you'll love Elijah and Sebastian.

And have you check out my True-Blue series yet?

You can start today with book one, LET ME SHOW YOU.

In the small town of Kirkby, there are busybodies, dogs who cause chaos, families who have the "best" of timing, and opportunities for good men to find their perfect match.

ACKNOWLEDGMENTS

A shout out to my amazing readers, especially those who love having paperback versions. You know who you are! :) Your support is everything!

ABOUT THE AUTHOR

I live and breathe all things book related. Usually with at least three books being read and two WiPs being written at the same time, life is merrily hectic. I tend to do nothing by halves, so I happily seek the craziness and busyness life offers.

Living on my small property in Queensland with my human family as well as my animal family of cows, chooks, and dogs, I really do appreciate the beauty of the world around me and am a believer that love truly is love.

To check for updates head to my website:
https://beccaseymour.com
https://landing.mailerlite.com/webforms/landing/r9f0i4
Plus, join my Facebook group, which I share with the awesome Louisa Masters here:
https://www.facebook.com/groups/rommancewithbeccalouisa/
On TikTok, follow me here: https://www.tiktok.com/@beccaseymourwrites

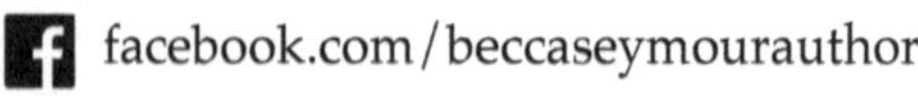

facebook.com/beccaseymourauthor

twitter.com/beccaseymour_

instagram.com/authorbeccaseymour

bookbub.com/authors/becca-seymour